Dedication

"This story is dedicated to my nine grandchildren. The laughter and enjoyment we have had in telling stories about the adventures of PūeDy the skunk have inspired me to publish them for other children to enjoy."

Order this book online at www.trafford.com/07-2379
or email orders@trafford.com

Most Trafford titles are also available at major online book retailers.

Note for Librarians: A cataloguing record for this book is available from Library and Archives Canada at www.collectionscanada.ca/amicus/index-e.html

Printed in Victoria, BC, Canada.

ISBN: 978-1-4251-5373-1

We at Trafford believe that it is the responsibility of us all, as both individuals and corporations, to make choices that are environmentally and socially sound. You, in turn, are supporting this responsible conduct each time you purchase a Trafford book, or make use of our publishing services. To find out how you are helping, please visit www.trafford.com/responsiblepublishing.html

Our mission is to efficiently provide the world's finest, most comprehensive book publishing service, enabling every author to experience success. To find out how to publish your book, your way, and have it available worldwide, visit us online at www.trafford.com/10510

 www.trafford.com

North America & international
toll-free: 1 888 232 4444 (USA & Canada)
phone: 250 383 6864 ♦ fax: 250 383 6804 ♦ email: info@trafford.com

The United Kingdom & Europe
phone: +44 (0)1865 722 113 ♦ local rate: 0845 230 9601
facsimile: +44 (0)1865 722 868 ♦ email: info.uk@trafford.com

10 9 8 7 6 5 4 3 2

It was a sunny spring afternoon. PūeDy is resting under the big red play house in the schoolyard. He is munching on a snack of lettuce and apple slices that the children left for him. They plan to meet after class and play together as they walk home from school. That is what they do almost every day.

You see- PūeDy is a very special little skunk. He lives with his mother and father in a cozy den at the edge of the great forest. He's a happy little fellow who loves to play with his animal friends and also with the children who live in the nearby village. He doesn't have a very bad smell like most skunks do and he has a special "gift" that enables him to talk to children and some times to grown ups too. After you first meet him, you soon come to know that PūeDy is very friendly and can do many things that other animals can not. The children know that they can play with him with no harm.

But the most special thing of all about PūeDy is - the **magical** power he has in his beautiful black and white striped tail.

PūeDy can use his tail to help him do all sorts of things. He can shape it into a tool to fix things or he can use it as a shovel or a rake.

He can even use it to enable him to fly.

Helping others and having fun are the two things that PūeDy likes to do most of all. But - should trouble appear, PūeDy can point his magic tail at danger and squirt at it with a **_smelly_** skunk mist to chase it away.

PūeDy and his animal pals Bobbin Robbin, Sniffer Rabbit, and Reddy Fox had spent the morning searching for food in the forest.

This is an important job. They save what they find to eat during the cold winter months ahead and store their food in a safe dry space at Reddy's den house.

All the animals have assigned chores in the hunt. Bobbin flies back and forth ahead to spot for food and find the best places to search. The others spread out and follow in a search line behind.

PūeDy uses his tail to dig out sweet roots and crack open the shells of any nuts they find. He then shapes his tail into a big box to carry their find back to Reddy's house. The team had very good luck this morning. They filled three baskets with wild cabbage, acorns and coneflower seeds that they found.

On the way back to Reddy's, they stopped to rest and get the news of the day at the tree home of Wisey Owl. Wisey talks with everyone in the forest. He always knows what is going on and keeps everyone informed. Today, he told them about a danger that exists from a fierce **Black Wolf** who has come down from the distant mountains to hunt

for food in the forest. When last seen, the wolf was lurking on the far side of the hill at the edge of the forest. He was chasing after all who came near. Wisey warned them to "stay away from that spot" for the "The Black Wolf is very nasty". He told them that "The wolf loves to eat little animals and even children for his dinner". They thanked Wisey for the warning and promised that "They would be very careful in their travels".

Just then - the school bell rings and PūeDy knows
that the children will come running out to play
with him. He loves to play with the children.
He tells them all about his adventures with the
animals in the forest and they tell him about what
they do in school.

On special days, like, "show and tell", the children's teacher lets them bring PūeDy into school with them. They even have made a special cage for him to stay in when he's there. PūeDy is always very good in school. He does not make noise and is especially careful not to leave any skunk smell behind before he goes home.

Today, the children plan to teach PūeDy how to jump rope. It takes a few turns for him to learn just when to jump and how high he has to go each time the rope comes by. Very soon, with some help from his tail, he is doing very well. The children laugh when PūeDy uses his tail to hover in the air and not come down for his next jump until the jump rope has made several swings.

The group had traveled about halfway through the woods when PūeDy hears a loud cry for – **Help!** It is coming from some of the children walking up ahead.

PūeDy rushes up to see what is the matter.

Crouched in the middle of the path in front of them is the fierce Black Wolf. His lips are pulled back in a snarl and his large white teeth are showing. He is growling loud and angrily and is about to pounce at them all. The children and PūeDy are in **danger!**

PūeDy immediately knows what to do.

He pushes his way past the frightened children and stands right in front of the startled wolf. He warns the wolf to "**Back away**"! But -it is too late! The wolf leaps at PūeDy and the children.

14

Just as the Black Wolf gets near him - PūeDy jumps to the side and **smacks** the wolf with his tail.

The wolf flies by and falls to the ground. After a moment he gets back up and leaps at PūeDy again.

This time PūeDy points his magic tail at the wolf and squirts him with one **huge** spray of very bad smelling skunk juice.

The Black Wolf is **stunned!**

He falls to the ground again. The skunk juice is so powerful that the wolf can not see. It is so smelly that the wolf can hardly breathe.

After a few moments the Black Wolf is able to get back up. He knows he has lost this battle. He turns and runs as fast as he can out of the forest and back to his home in the mountain.

PūeDy is a hero. He has saved the children and the animals in the forest from the fierce Black Wolf. Every one is pleased. "Three cheers for PūeDy!" shout the children! ***"Hip- Hip- Hooray! Hip-Hip- Hooray! Hip-Hip- Hooray***!" Then they lift him up on their shoulders and carry him away in celebration.

Wisey has been perched nearby in a tall tree watching all of this happen. He flies off to spread the good news to all the animals in the forest.

The children carry PūeDy home so that he can tell his mother and father about his adventure. His mother is so proud of him that she promises to make his favorite meal of steamed cabbage for dinner. She tells PūeDy that "He can invite his animal friends to celebrate with them"

That night Bobbin, Reddy, Sniffer and Wisey come over to join in the celebration dinner. They bring a special dessert of wild honey pudding that they have made for all to share.

The next day PūeDy is honored by the children and their teacher at school. They hang a gold medal on a ribbon around his neck and decorate his cage with a sign that reads- *"PūeDy Skunk Our Hero"*.

It was a grand time for all! – The End